DISNEY'S

DouG™

Created by
Jim Jinkins

CHRONICLES

Doug and the
End of the
World

by Dennis Garvey and Tommy Nichols

Illustrated by
William Presing, Vinh Truong,
and Sophie Kittredge

Doug and the End of the World is hand-illustrated by the same
Grade A Quality Jumbo artists who bring you
Disney's Doug, the television series.

JUMBO
PICTURES
INC.

GRADE A QUALITY

DISNEY
PRESS

New York

Original characters for "The Funnies" developed by
Jim Jinkins and Joe Aaron.

Printed in Mexico.

1 3 5 7 9 10 8 6 4 2

The artwork for this book is prepared using watercolor.

The text for this book is set in 18-point New Century Schoolbook.

Library of Congress Catalog Card Number: 99-60524

ISBN: 0-7868-4300-4

For more Disney Press fun, visit www.DisneyBooks.com

Disney's

DouG™

Created by
Jim Jinkins

CHRONICLES

Doug and the End of the World

CHAPTER ONE

"Does that mean I shouldn't use hair spray anymore?" Beebe asked nervously.

Professor Ogee wrinkled his brow. "If it contains fluorocarbons, it's not a very good idea. Aerosols can be very destructive to the ozone layer."

"Well, an unattractive hairstyle can be very destructive to a girl's

social life," Beebe replied. The whole science class laughed.

Except Doug. He thought for a moment, then raised his hand. "Is there anything we can do to help save the ozone layer?"

Professor Ogee smiled. "I'm glad you asked that, Doug. It just so happens that for your next science project I'd like you to come up with ways to help save our planet. I'm sure you all will think of some great ideas."

Just then, the bell rang. As the kids gathered their books, Roger called out to Doug and Skeeter. "Hey, Funnie! I know a great way you and Valentine can save the planet!"

"Yeah, what's that?" Doug asked.

"Get off at the next stop," Roger cackled, sauntering out of the classroom.

"Oh, yeah?" Doug called after him.

"This planet doesn't make stops, Roger. It's express all the way!" Skeeter honked. "Let's go to Swirly's. All this ozone talk is making me thirsty."

CHAPTER TWO

Everyone at Swirly's was talking about the ozone layer. Doug, Skeeter, Skunky, and Patti sat at a booth drinking Frothy Goats. Al and Moo Sleech leaned over the back of the next booth and joined the conversation.

"I wouldn't be too concerned about the ozone layer if I were you," Al said brightly.

Moo continued, "Yes, we learned all about it at the Moody School for the Gifted, and there are many worse things that could happen!" Moo's eyes glistened with excitement at all the gloomy possibilities. "There's pollution everywhere around us, and plenty of global warming to cook it all up. And us with it!"

Al nodded in agreement. "And don't forget the melting polar ice caps! Who's gonna care about the ozone when the whole planet is submerged under a tidal wave?"

Doug squirmed uncomfortably in his seat, swallowing a Tater Twistie whole. He wasn't enjoying this conversation. "It can't really be that bad, can it?" Doug asked hopefully.

"Not as bad as killer bees," Skeeter interjected. "K-BLUF said they're heading our way from the tropical rain forest. And boy, are they mad!"

"Yeah, I guess they would be," said Patti. "After all, a thousand acres of the rain forest are being destroyed every day. I read that it's causing whole new diseases to spread."

Doug pushed away his plate. "Gee, there are so many ways the earth is in danger."

"Whoa, dude, that's nothing," Skunky said. "Dormant volcanoes, man. Erupting. *Kaboom!* Hot lava. Rocks. We're cooked. Like, what if Mount Saint Buster decided to blow? Whoa!"

Roger Klotz, standing nearby, laughed. "Oh, brother, what a bunch of crybabies! You guys haven't even thought of the most dangerous thing of all." Roger paused, then added, "The sewers of Bluffington are full of alligators!"

The kids all burst out laughing. "Really, Roger?" Patti asked. "Isn't that just some old superstition?"

Roger leaned over the booth and whispered, "Are you kidding? Six years ago I had a baby alligator that I accidentally flushed down the toilet. "Where do you think he is now? And how big must he be? And how many others are down there with him?" Roger pointed to the floor and shook his head knowingly. "They oughta be coming up looking for food any minute now. A nice Funnie burger or some Valentine Twisties!"

As Roger walked away, laughing, Al Sleech spoke up. "There

really isn't anything to worry about, you know."

Doug looked hopeful. "There isn't? Really?"

Moo exchanged a look with his brother and said, "Of course not! Al and I have already made contact with an alien civilization. There's a spaceship on its way, even as we speak, that will remove us from harm's way."

Before anybody had time to react to that bit of news, Connie burst through the front door of Swirly's. She waved a flyer and cried, "Look! The Beets are coming! The Beets are coming!"

Connie put the flyer on the table

and squeezed in beside Patti. "It's this weekend in Lucky Duck Park!"

The bright, blue flyer screamed the words BEET'S THIRD ANNUAL FINAL FAREWELL CONCERT. "This is so cool!" crowed Skeeter. "We've gotta go!"

As the kids began to buzz with enthusiasm, Doug sat quietly, wondering how everybody could forget so quickly all the dangers they had just discussed. Patti nudged him. "Isn't this great, Doug? We can all go together."

Doug sighed. "Yeah, sure, I guess so."

As the kids exchanged high

fives and happily made plans for the concert, Doug looked out the window at the sky and muttered, almost to himself, "If there still *is* a world on Saturday."

CHAPTER THREE

Later, at home, Doug paced
around the living room, with
Porkchop right behind him.

"I don't get it, Porkchop. The
world could end any day now, and
nobody seems to care."

Porkchop shrugged as Doug sat
down on the couch. "I just don't
get it." Doug sighed.

As Doug lay his head on the

arm of the couch, he began to daydream. . . .

Doug raced through Bluffington as the sounds of explosions roared and smoke filled the air. Mount Saint Buster was erupting with a great burst of lava and fire!

Startled, Doug saw Patti with her beetball bat, shagging rocks as they flew out of the volcano. "Hey, Doug," Patti cried happily. "What a great way to get in some batting practice! Wanna join me?"

Doug shook his head, bewildered, and walked away. He jerked his head up when he heard the sound of rushing water, and scurried up a tree just in time to avoid a tidal

wave that was pouring down the
street. As the wave passed, he
saw Skunky surfing on top of it.
"Whoa, dude!" Skunky shouted.
"Waves are breaking big today.
Totally torque, man!"

After the wave passed
by, Doug ran into Lucky
Duck Park. Out of
breath, he
sat on a
bench and
noticed
Beebe sitting
beside
him,
holding a
sun

reflector under her face. "Oh, hi, Doug," Beebe said brightly. "Since that pesky old ozone layer is gone, a girl can finally get a decent tan in a matter of seconds. Isn't it great?"

Upset, Doug raced out of the park and headed to his best friend Skeeter's house. Surely Skeeter would understand how bad things really were. As an earthquake rocked the house, Doug walked in Skeeter's back door. He was stunned to see Skeeter sitting calmly in the kitchen, eating waffles as a swarm of bees circled the room, buzzing menacingly.

Skeeter smiled. "Hey, Doug, want some waffles? They're great with this killer-bee honey!" Skeeter held up a spoon of honey totally covered with bees. Bees swarmed all around Skeeter's head as Doug backed out the door.

As he stepped out the back door of Skeeter's house, he saw a spacecraft hovering overhead. A hatch opened and Al and Moo stuck their heads out. "Greetings, Doug! Care to join us and our intergalactic friends as we escape this earthly doom?"

Doug leaned against the porch railing, speechless.

CHAPTER FOUR

Doug snapped out of his day-dream with a start. "Oh, no! Maybe I am the only one who cares!" As he sat on the couch with his head in his hands, his mother, Theda, came in from the kitchen. "Why, Douglas, what's the matter? You look so sad."

Doug sighed. "Nothing, Mom, except there are so many ways

the world could end and nobody seems to be worried about it but me."

Theda sat down beside Doug and put her arm around him. "Oh, Doug, worrying isn't going to help anything. Besides, there's plenty to look forward to. Why, we're starting a brand-new project tomorrow at the Dejavu Recycling Center. Maybe you'd like to help!"

Doug shook his head. "No thanks, Mom. I have a science project due next week."

Theda stood up and started back to the kitchen. "Well, don't you worry about the world. It's been around for a long time and it hasn't gone anywhere yet. I'm making your favorite dinner . . . beanie weanie olé! That's something to look forward to, isn't it?"

Doug smiled as Theda returned to the kitchen. Good old Mom, she always knew what to say. Maybe she was right. Maybe things weren't so bad after all. Doug turned on the TV and was totally psyched to see that a Smash Adams movie was on. But a news bulletin broke into the broadcast. "Leading scientists have just announced that a huge asteroid is hurtling toward Earth." The announcer continued, "The asteroid, named Shimmy Koko Bopp, is expected to hit within the next few years, probably wiping out civilization as we know it. And now back to our regular program."

Doug jumped up from the sofa in a panic. "Things *aren't* as bad as I thought they were! They're worse!"

CHAPTER FIVE

Early the next day, Doug was on his way to Swirly's. He had barely slept the night before, dreaming about a big giant asteroid careening toward Earth.

As he proceeded down the street, he came upon Skunky, bent over, pointing a handheld, battery-operated fan at the sidewalk. "What are you doing, Skunky?" Doug asked.

Skunky looked up and replied, "Science project! I've solved global warming, whoa! What's yours, dude?"

Doug shrugged. "I don't know yet."

Skunky hurried away, still bent over his fan. "Gotta go, man! Gotta cool off more ground before that asteroid hits it."

As Doug headed in the opposite direction, a limousine stopped alongside him. The rear window rolled down and Beebe stuck her head out. "Hey, Doug!"

Doug noticed that Beebe's hair

was hanging down straight and limp. "Oh, hey, Beebe! You look kinda different."

"It's my science project," Beebe replied. "I'm saving the ozone layer by not using hair spray. Oh, the sacrifices a girl has to make to save her planet! See you at the Beets' concert tomorrow."

"Yeah, sure, Beebe," Doug said weakly.

As Doug waved to the limo, he was suddenly bumped from behind. "Oh, sorry, Doug, I didn't see you there," said Chalky breathlessly. "I was practicing my broken field running."

Doug asked, "Do you have a big game coming up?"

"No, this is my science project. Maybe we can't stop asteroids from hitting the earth, but we don't have to let them hit us!" Chalky continued zigzagging up the street.

When Doug walked into Swirly's, he saw Skeeter in a booth with Al and Moo. The Sleeches were showing Skeeter elaborate charts and graphs, mapping out the route they planned to take on their space journey to safety.

"You see, Skeeter," Al was saying, "by the time the asteroid smashes into this planet, we'll have already crossed into a completely different solar system! It's foolproof!"

Moo nodded. "And there's no reason at all why our alien friends would object to taking you, too."

Skeeter scratched his head. "I
don't know, guys. I kinda like this
solar system. Hey, there's Doug!"

Doug joined them at the table.
As he sat down, he saw Roger
through the window, waving
his arms and yelling at some

construction workers. "What's up with Roger?" Doug asked.

"Oh, that's his science project," Skeeter told him. "He's having an underground shelter built. An underground mansion, actually, complete with a bowling alley and an indoor swimming pool."

Al laughed derisively. "Underground mansion! As if being trapped inside the earth is going to help when the tidal wave hits!"

Moo slapped the table. "Yes, the whole town will be his swimming pool then." Al and Moo laughed as Doug got up from the table.

"Gotta go, guys," he said, hurrying out of Swirly's. He

couldn't stand to listen to any more talk about disaster.

Doug walked through Lucky Duck Park. As he came out the other side, he saw his mother and a team of Dejavu volunteers hard at work in the vacant lot across from the park. Theda waved and Doug walked over to her.

"Oh, Douglas, isn't it wonderful?" Theda beamed. She gestured at the lot, which had always been filled with junk. The Dejavu workers had built a jungle gym out of some old stair banisters, and, in another corner, they were busily turning old hot water heaters into park benches.

"Yeah, that's great, Mom," Doug said halfheartedly. Then he saw a worker take off a welding mask. It was Patti!

"Hey, Doug!" Patti called as she ran over to him. "Did you come to help?" She stopped when she saw how miserable Doug looked. "What's the matter, Doug?"

Doug and Patti sat down next to each other on some old rubber

tires. Doug knew that if anyone
would understand the way he
felt, it would be Patti.

"I don't know, Patti, the play-
ground looks great, but I can't
understand why anyone would

even bother, what with the asteroid coming and everything. Am I the only one who cares?" Doug sighed.

"Gee, Doug," Patti replied sympathetically, "I've been thinking about the asteroid. Everybody is. But what can we do? It's not supposed to reach Earth for years, and anything could happen by then. We might as well make the most out of each day and just hope for the best, right?"

Patti jumped up and put her welding mask back on. "I'd better get back to work. See you at the concert tomorrow?"

Doug tried to smile. "Yeah, see

ya tomorrow." He walked away, sorry he had missed the chance to spend the day working with Patti. This worrying about the future was really messing up the present.

CHAPTER SIX

That evening, Doug sat at his desk, deep in thought. At least his friends were making some effort, but Doug realized that it was going to take a lot more than handheld fans and flat hair to save the planet.

Doug's father stuck his head into the room. "Hey, son! Let's all go to dinner at Cowpoke Pete's

Porketeria. How fast can you be ready?"

Doug shook his head. "No thanks, Dad. I'm not hungry, and I've got to work on my science project. I'll just have a hot dog later with Porkchop."

As the family left for dinner, Doug doodled in his notebook. What would Quailman do in a case like this? . . .

The streets of Megalopolis were filled with people. They had just heard that an asteroid was about to destroy their fair city. As citizens scrambled for safety, a woman cried out, "Help us, Quailman, wherever you are!"

In the Thicket of Solitude, Quailman and Quaildog were playing chess. "Jumping Jupiter! You win again, Quaildog." Suddenly Quailman's super-sensitive hearing picked up the cries for help from Megalopolis. It sounded like a phone was ringing. "Hark! I wonder what the problem is."

Quaildog tugged on Quailman's cape and pointed skyward. Quailman looked up and exclaimed, "Why, if I'm not mistaken, that asteroid seems to be hurtling right toward this planet! But no time for that now, Quaildog! We must fly off to see what has the citizens in such an uproar."

As Quailman soared away, Quaildog shrugged and made his "Oh, brother!" expression before taking off after him.

As the heroes reached Megalopolis, the shadow of the asteroid was darkening the entire city. "I've got it, Quaildog! We can escort these good citizens out of harm's way to our home planet! They'll be safe on planet Bob!"

At Quailman's direction, the
citizens of Megalopolis all joined
hands in a gigantic chain. As
Quailman took the hand of the
first citizen, he shouted, "We're
off, with the speed of the
Quail!"

With Quailman leading and Quaildog holding the hand of the last citizen in the line, they flew off toward planet Bob, narrowly missing the plummeting asteroid!

CHAPTER SEVEN

Doug was startled out of his Quailman fantasy when his family came home from dinner. His mother came into his room and said, "Oh, Doug, I'm sorry you didn't come with us. Dinner was delicious, and we met that nice young singer you like so much. Chip? No, Cheap . . ."

Doug was shocked. "You don't mean Chap Lipman?"

Theda smiled. "Yes, I believe that was it. And three others, Munroe something, a girl named Wendy, and a strange young man named Flounder . . ."

"The Beets?!" Doug shouted. "I can't believe it. You met the Beets?"

"They sat at the table next to us," Theda explained. "And they were so nice. We went to their rehearsal after we had dessert. They're giving a concert tomorrow in the park."

"I know." Doug moaned. "You mean you went to their private

rehearsal?" Porkchop slapped his paw to his forehead and fainted.

"Yes, the whole family. We tried to call, but you didn't answer the phone. Have you eaten, Douglas? I brought you a doggie bag, and one for Porkchop, too."

Doug slumped his head on his desk. "No thanks, Mom," he said. "I don't feel like eating. Ever."

As Theda left the room, Doug took the globe off his desk and twirled it on his finger. "Oh, man!

Even if the world *is* ending, it would have been really cool to hang out with the Beets like that!"

CHAPTER EIGHT

That night, Doug tossed and turned as his dream took him back to Megalopolis. . . .

"Here we are, folks. Planet Bob! You'll be safe here while Quaildog and I save the earth. Fly away, Quaildog!"

Quailman and Quaildog arrived just before the asteroid entered Earth's atmosphere. "We must deflect that asteroid, Quaildog. But how? I know! Quail logic! But time is running out, so I must be brief." Quailman paused a moment, then snapped his fingers. "Brief! That's it, Quaildog! My Power Briefs!"

Removing Quailman's Power Briefs, Quailman and Quaildog each took hold of the waistband and flew in opposite directions above the city. The Power Briefs, stretched like a slingshot, caught the asteroid and sent it hurtling into space.

"We did it, Quaildog!" Quailman cheered. The superheroes hovered triumphantly, savoring their

moment of glory. Quaildog suddenly tugged on Quailman's cape,
pointing upward.

"Yes, Quaildog," Quailman
gloated. "The asteroid is hurtling
away . . . away . . . *right toward
planet Bob!*"

Quailman and Quaildog took off at top quail-speed and flew past the asteroid. Landing on planet Bob as the shadow of the asteroid loomed above, Quailman and Quaildog once again organized the citizens of Megalopolis into a chain to fly away. Just as Quaildog, again bringing up the rear, took off, he reached out and caught the asteroid, which was now no larger than a marble.

"Nice catch, Quaildog," Quailman called. "I guess all that hurtling through atmospheres vaporized the asteroid! Now it's nothing but hot gravel. And a dandy souvenir."

Quaildog gave Quailman a
thumbs-up sign as Quailman
shouted, "The people of
Megalopolis are safe once again!"

CHAPTER NINE

When Doug woke up Saturday
morning, the sun shone brightly
and birds chirped outside his
window. He rubbed his eyes and
said to Porkchop, "You know,
Porkchop, maybe things aren't so
bad after all. Let's get ready to
see the Beets!"

When Doug and Porkchop got
downstairs, Mom and Dad were

sitting at the kitchen table. Phil was reading the *Bluffington Gazette*. "Good morning, Douglas," Theda said. "Ready for breakfast?"

"Sure, Mom," Doug replied. "I'm so hungry I could . . . huh?" Doug stopped in midsentence as he noticed the headline on his dad's newspaper: ASTEROID NOT HEADING FOR EARTH AFTER ALL!

"I can't believe it! The asteroid isn't going to hit us?" Doug asked, astonished.

Phil chuckled. "No, it turns out that a scientist forgot to carry the 0, and it'll miss the earth by

5.914 billion kilometers. They're a little concerned about Pluto . . ."

Theda brought Doug a big plate of pancakes. "Now, Phil, the

scientists said they're really, really sorry. Anybody can make a mistake," she said. "Don't you feel better now, Doug?"

Doug smiled. "I sure do. I could eat 5.914 billion pancakes—one for each mile away from Shimmy Koko Bopp. I guess I got my appetite back."

Later that day, on their way to the concert, Doug told Porkchop, "Boy, I wasted all that time worrying about something that's not even going to happen. Patti was right. You gotta just make the most of each day and hope for the best."

Porkchop nodded in agreement.

Just then, they passed the vacant lot that Theda's volunteers had recycled into a beautiful new park. "That's it! I know what I can do!" Doug exclaimed.

"Come on, Porkchop!" Doug called as he took off running. "We've got to borrow some stuff from Mom's recycling center!"

CHAPTER TEN

The Beets had never sounded better. As their music filled the park, Doug and his friends danced and sang along with every song, right in front of the stage.

As the crowd began leaving after the last encore, Skeeter said, "Man, that was awesome!"

Doug agreed. "I can't wait until their next farewell concert!"

Patti smiled. "I'm glad to see you're acting like your old self again," she said. "You must be glad that asteroid isn't going to hit us after all."

Doug nodded happily as Beebe said, "Yeah, but we still have to worry about ozone layers and that other stuff."

"Worrying won't help, Beebe," Doug told her, as he reached into a large bag and pulled out a bunch of sticks with points to pick up litter. "We're all still here, so we might as well do whatever we can to make things better."

Doug handed each of his friends a stick and a garbage bag. He

pointed to the now-empty park,
which was strewn with trash left
by the concert-goers. "First one to
fill up a trash bag gets a shake at
Swirly's, my treat!"